# REGINALD GOES TO THE MALL

WRITTEN BY
KATHERINE RAWSON

ILLUSTRATED BY
MAX STASIUK

PIONEER VALLEY EDUCATIONAL PRESS, INC.

# CONTENTS

# CHAPTER 1
# OUT THE DOOR

Reginald sat in the kitchen,
eagerly wagging his tail.
Amy and Jack were putting
on their jackets.
Their mother was picking
up her car keys.
Their father was telling
everyone to hurry.

All this could mean only one thing.
They were going for a car ride!

5

Reginald loved car rides. He loved sitting in the back seat between Amy and Jack. He loved feeling the breeze ruffle his fur when the window was open. He didn't care where the car took him —
he just loved the ride.
Reginald waited by the front door, wagging his tail wildly.

"Silly Reginald," said Amy, patting the top of his head.
"We are going to the mall.
Dogs aren't allowed there.
You stay and wait for us here, and we'll play with you when we get home."

"We'll bring you a treat
from the mall pet store,"
Jack promised.

Reginald watched through the door as his family got in the car. He listened to the car doors shut. He watched sadly as the car backed out of the driveway. Reginald jumped up to lean his front paws against the door and get a closer look.

Creeeaak! The door suddenly swung open under his weight,
and Reginald was outside, standing on the front step. Reginald bounded across the yard and up the street, running after the car.

The car drove quickly out of sight, but Reginald kept going. He ran past the neighbors' houses.

Children called out to him
from their yards. "Hi, Reginald!
Come play with us!" But Reginald
didn't stop. He wasn't interested
in playing right now. He was only
interested in getting to the mall.
He wanted to find Amy and Jack!

## CHAPTER 2
## DUMPSTER!

Reginald kept racing along the road. Soon he wasn't passing houses or yards. Instead, the sides of the street were filled with store after store after store. After a while, he came to a huge store with a large parking lot in front of it. A sign over the wide glass doors read: **Supermarket**.

# SUPERMARKET

## ENTRANCE

Reginald couldn't read the sign, but he knew the store. He had been to the supermarket before. He had never been inside, but he had been behind it, where there was something Reginald loved. It was a giant dumpster!

Reginald ran quickly across the parking lot and around the building to the back. There was the dumpster with its lid wide open, and it was overflowing with garbage. "Yum!" thought Reginald. He jumped up on top of the garbage heap in the dumpster.

Reginald sniffed deeply. He was certain there were some meaty bones somewhere! He eagerly began to dig through the garbage. He dug through rotting bananas and soggy cardboard. He dug through moldy bread, smashed tomatoes, and stale pie. He dug through half-eaten sandwiches and wilted salads. Only his tail was visible at the top of the heap. Reginald's tail wagged wildly when he finally found what he was looking for in the pile of garbage.

"Bones!" thought Reginald.
Reginald loved bones.
He gnawed and gnawed
as he happily wagged his tail.
He was so busy chomping on bones
that he didn't hear the sound
of footsteps as they came  near.

"Get out of there, you stinky
mutt!" yelled a gruff voice.

The bones were delicious,
and Reginald kept gnawing.

"I said get out!" said the voice
again, and Reginald felt a sharp
yank on his tail.

"Owwooooo!" yelped Reginald
as he backed out of the garbage
heap. He jumped down
to the pavement and scurried away
as fast as he could go.

# CHAPTER 3
# PERFUME

Reginald didn't slow down
until he reached the street.
His tail was a bit sore, but he didn't
mind. He felt happy remembering
the delicious bones he had been
gnawing. He didn't notice
the banana peel hanging on his ear.
He didn't see the blueberry stains
covering his fur. And he wasn't
aware of the odor of garbage
that followed him wherever he went.

But everyone else smelled it!

A woman stepped out of a bookstore. "Hello, nice doggy," she said when she saw Reginald. And then, "Oh! What a horrible smell! Oh my!" Gasping, she fled back into the store.

"Mommy, I'm going to pet that doggy," said a little boy getting out of a car. And then, "Ewwwww! I'm not touching that stinky dog!" He jumped back in the car and rolled up the windows.

"What a reek!"

"Ghastly stink!"

Up and down the street, people ran into stores or closed their car windows as Reginald walked by. But Reginald didn't care. He only cared about getting to the mall and finding Amy and Jack.

Soon, Reginald saw a huge white building in front of him. The large glass doors opened automatically when he approached. He stepped inside, and cool air, soft lights, and gentle music greeted him. He was in the largest department store in the mall, he was right in front of the perfume counter.

Reginald took a deep sniff.
"Mmmm!" he thought.

"This is our most popular scent,"
said the lady behind the counter,
holding up a small glass bottle.

Her customer took a whiff.
"Why, it's disgusting!" The customer
choked and grimaced.
"It smells just like a stinky dog
that's been playing in the garbage."

The saleslady and the customer
turned and glared at Reginald.

"Get out of here, you awful,
stinky mutt!" shouted the perfume
lady. "Go on. Go outside."
She shooed Reginald away
with a fly swatter while pinching
her nose.

Reginald turned and ran,
but he didn't run toward
the big glass doors. Instead,
he scampered through the whole
department store, running
until he got to a doorway
at the opposite end.

# CHAPTER 4
# REGINALD GOES SHOPPING

Reginald found himself in the
middle of the mall. He stopped
running to catch his breath
and look around.
He saw people walking
around in pairs and small groups.
He saw people carrying large bags
and stopping to look in store
windows. He saw people riding
up and down the escalator,
and he saw people resting
on benches.

But he didn't see Amy
and Jack anywhere.

There were brightly lit stores all around him. As Reginald walked along, he looked in the store windows. He saw displays of shoes and dishes and clothes and toys. He saw shoppers everywhere, but he didn't see Amy and Jack.

Then Reginald saw a store with
an interesting display in the window.
There was sports equipment
like bats and helmets and gloves
and pads. Reginald also saw
something he loved to play with!
"Woof!" he barked and ran
into the store.

All the shoppers turned
to stare as Reginald ran
into the window display
to play with the soccer ball.

"What an awful stink!"

"Air! Give me air! I think
I'm going to faint!"

Shoppers, gasping for breath,
ran out of the store.
Reginald didn't pay any attention.
All he wanted was the soccer ball.
He grabbed it and chased it back
into the middle of the mall.

Reginald trotted along with
the ball clenched in his teeth.
He stopped to shake it and growl,
then looked around for someone
to play with. A friendly-looking girl
was standing in front of the jewelry
store. Reginald dropped the ball
at her feet and waited for her
to kick it to him.

"Ohhh!" cried the girl. "What's that terrible smell? Daddy! Get me away from that stinky dog!" Her father scooped her up and ran towards the exit.

People turned to see
what the commotion was about.
They saw Reginald sitting calmly
with a soccer ball in front of him.
Then they smelled him.

"Ewwwww! Disgusting!"

"Nasty, nasty stink."

"Repulsive!"

Everyone pinched their noses
and ran out of the mall.
There was no one to play with Reginald
and the soccer ball, so he picked
it up and stepped onto the escalator.

As he neared the top, a pleasant
odor drifted by his nose. Reginald
smelled pizza, french fries, and hot
apple pie.

# CHAPTER 5
# COME GET YOUR STINKY DOG!

Reginald followed the delicious smell through the mall until he came to the food court. Then he just stood and sniffed.

There was food everywhere. There were bowls of chili, fried chicken, and hot dogs with mustard. There were pretzels and donuts and steak sandwiches. Reginald saw every kind of food he could ever imagine.

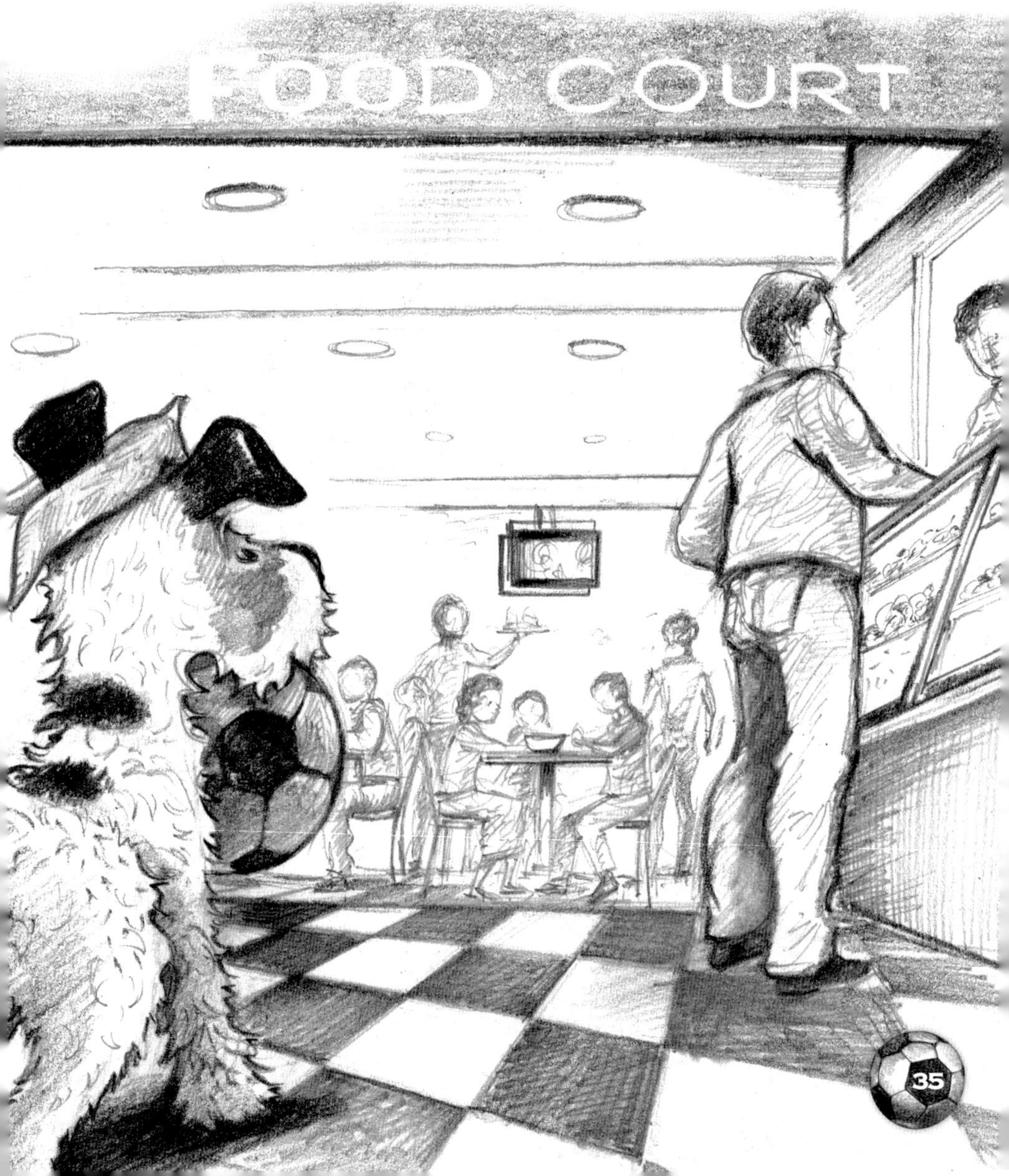
FOOD COURT

Everything looked so good
and smelled so delicious! Reginald
didn't know what to look at
or where to go first.
And the people were so busy eating
that no one noticed Reginald.

But then they smelled him.

"What stinks so much?"

"It's awful. Somebody open
a window!"

"It's that stinky dog over there."

People stopped eating
and glared at Reginald.
Then they pushed their chairs back
and ran out of the food court,
gasping for fresh air.

Suddenly, the food court
was empty, and there was no one
left to enjoy all that food. No one,
that is, except Reginald. He jumped
up on the nearest table and began
to eat.

Reginald was so busy licking
the plates clean, he didn't hear
any footsteps behind him.
But suddenly he felt a hand
grab his collar.

"Got him!" said a gruff voice.

Reginald turned his head
and saw two security officers
wearing gas masks. One of them
was holding him by the collar.

"What should we do
with him now?"

"He's too stinky to take
to the office. Put him in that closet
over there. I'll go return
the soccer ball he took."

The other officer dragged Reginald
to a closet and shoved him inside.

Now Reginald was alone inside the dark closet. He couldn't see anything. He heard the officers' footsteps as they walked away, and then everything was quiet.

A minute later, a loud voice could be heard everywhere in the mall. "We have a stinky dog near the security office. Will the owner please come get your dog? Now!"

# CHAPTER 6
# A SURPRISE FOR REGINALD

Reginald heard footsteps coming toward the closet. Then he heard familiar voices. "Amy and Jack!" Reginald thought. He had found them at last.

The door swung open. Reginald bounded out and jumped all over Amy and Jack, licking their faces.

"You're stinky," said Amy, pushing him away and pinching her nose.

Jack said, "We knew the announcement was about you when they said they had a stinky dog."

The security officer said, "You'll have to take your dog home right away."

Amy and Jack looked at their parents. "How can we?" said Amy. "He'll stink up the car."

"Then we'll have to take the car to the car wash," said Jack.

"That's a great idea," said their father. "Let's do it."

"Do what?" Jack asked.

"You'll see. Come with me."

Reginald followed Amy and Jack and their parents as they walked through the mall with their hands over their noses. They went out the big glass doors and across the street. There, they saw a big sign. It read: **Car Wash**.

"Wait for me here," said their father. He went into the office. In a few minutes, a man came out. He was pulling a little wagon behind him.

"Come on, boy," he said
to Reginald. Reginald jumped into
the wagon, and the man pulled
it over to the car wash entrance.
He gave it a little shove, and
Reginald and the little wagon
went into the car wash.

As the wagon moved along,
jets of water and soap sprayed
all over Reginald. Next, huge
brushes scrubbed his back and sides.
How good it felt! Then more sprays
of water washed away the soap
and dirt. Finally, warm air blew
his fur dry.

When Reginald came out the other end of the car wash, his fur was fluffy and he smelled clean and sweet.

Amy and Jack hugged him. "We got you something at the mall," said Jack. He reached into his shopping bag and pulled out a soccer ball.

"Woof!" barked Reginald. He jumped up and grabbed the ball in his teeth.

"Let's go home,"
said Amy and Jack's mother.

Amy and Jack followed
their parents back to their car.
Reginald trotted happily behind them,
carrying his new soccer ball
in his mouth.